ower of Energy (Stride) (Library Binding)

Oil Power

Introduces readers to what oil power is, how it is today and how it might be used in the future, an benefits and drawbacks of this energy source. Addi features include a table of conten...

#2310524 P. Richards   Available:01/01/2023   32 pgs
Grade:234 Dewey:665   LEX:760

Solar Power $23.95

Introduces readers to what solar power is, how it is used today and how it might be used in the future, and the benefits and drawbacks of this energy source. Additional features include a table of cont...

#2310525 L. Perdew   Available:01/01/2023   32 pgs
Grade:234 Dewey:621   LEX:780

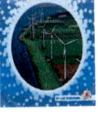
Wind Power $23.95

Introduces readers to what wind power is, how it is used today and how it might be used in the future, and the benefits and drawbacks of this energy source. Additional features include a table of conte...

#2310526 L. Harkrader   Available:01/01/2023   32 pgs
Grade:234 Dewey:621   LEX:770

Hydroelectric Power

BY LAURA PERDEW

Stride

An Imprint of The Child's World®
childsworld.com

Published by The Child's World®
800-599-READ • childsworld.com

Copyright © 2023 by The Child's World®
All rights reserved. No part of this book may be reproduced or utilized in any form or by any means without written permission from the publisher.

Photography Credits
Photographs ©: Sean Pavone/Shutterstock Images, cover, 1; Opis Zagreb/Shutterstock Images, 5; Everett Collection/Shutterstock Images, 6; Vlad G./Shutterstock Images, 7; Shutterstock Images, 8, 9, 25, 26, 28; Ded Mityay/Shutterstock Images, 11; Claudia Otte/Shutterstock Images, 13; Alexey Kamenskiy/Shutterstock Images, 14; Olenka Kotyk/Shutterstock Images, 15; Warren A. Metcalf/iStockphoto, 17; John Dvorak/Shutterstock Images, 19; iStockphoto, 20; Sean Lema/Shutterstock Images, 21; J.W. Cohen/Shutterstock Images, 22

ISBN Information
9781503864979 (Reinforced Library Binding)
9781503865976 (Portable Document Format)
9781503866812 (Online Multi-user eBook)
9781503867659 (Electronic Publication)

LCCN 2022939516

Printed in the United States of America

ABOUT THE AUTHOR
Laura Perdew is a mom, writing consultant, and author of more than 40 books for children. She lives and plays in Boulder, Colorado.

Contents

CHAPTER ONE
Making Water Work . . . 4

CHAPTER TWO
Positive Impacts of Hydropower . . . 10

CHAPTER THREE
Negative Impacts of Hydropower . . . 16

CHAPTER FOUR
The Future of Hydropower . . . 24

GLOSSARY . . . 30

FAST FACTS . . . 31

ONE STRIDE FURTHER . . . 31

FIND OUT MORE . . . 32

INDEX . . . 32

CHAPTER ONE

Making Water Work

When water is in motion, it can be powerful. The energy created by moving or falling water is called hydroelectric power, or hydropower. More than 2,000 years ago, people began using this power to help them do work. The ancient Greeks and Romans used water to turn waterwheels. This helped them grind grain into flour. Hydropower was also used in ancient China. People used it for grinding and papermaking. By the 1000s, waterwheels were used across Europe. Later, people took this technology to the Americas. Grain and lumber mills were built next to rivers. In the 1800s, fabric factories used water **turbines**. This was a new type of waterwheel. It turned a system of gears, wheels, and more. This system powered the devices used to make fabric.

Some waterwheels were built thousands of years ago in Syria. They were called norias. They had wooden buckets on the edges that collected water from the river as the wheel turned.

Hydropower was important for factories in the 1800s and 1900s. Water turbines powered machines that spun cotton or wool into thread. Cloth could be made much faster than before. This changed the way people in factories worked.

In the second half of the 1800s, people discovered that water could be used to create electricity. In 1882, the first hydroelectric plant in the world began making electricity. It was in Wisconsin. By the end of the century, many other plants like it were built.

Hydropower uses the **kinetic energy** of moving water. On a waterwheel, the force of moving water pushes paddles on the wheel. This makes the wheel rotate. The rotating shaft at the center of the wheel transfers the energy to other machines.

Generating electricity works in a similar way. At power plants, moving water turns blades in a turbine. The turbine spins a **generator** that makes electricity.

Sometimes a power plant simply uses the force of a river's flow. Water is taken from the river to flow to the hydropower turbines. The water is then returned to the river. This is called a diversion system. Other power plants use a storage system. A dam is built to create a **reservoir**. Water is released through the hydropower turbines.

NIAGARA FALLS
Niagara Falls is on the border of New York and Ontario, Canada. It is on the Niagara River, between Lake Ontario and Lake Erie. Niagara Falls has three waterfalls. This makes it the second-largest waterfall in the world. In the late 1800s, people understood the falls' potential to generate electricity. In 1895, a power plant opened there. It is now one of five power plants along the river. These plants deliver electricity to cities in New York and Ontario.

The Hoover Dam hydroelectric plant has 17 water turbines. Water flows to the turbines through pipes and makes them spin. This sets off a system of gears, magnets, and wires, powering an electric generator.

The water is used to create electricity. Then the water returns to the river below the dam.

Another type of power plant uses a pumped-storage system. Water is pumped from a water source up to a reservoir at a higher location. When demand for electricity is high, the stored water is released. Water passes through hydropower turbines below the reservoir. This makes electricity.

HOW A HYDROELECTRIC DAM WORKS

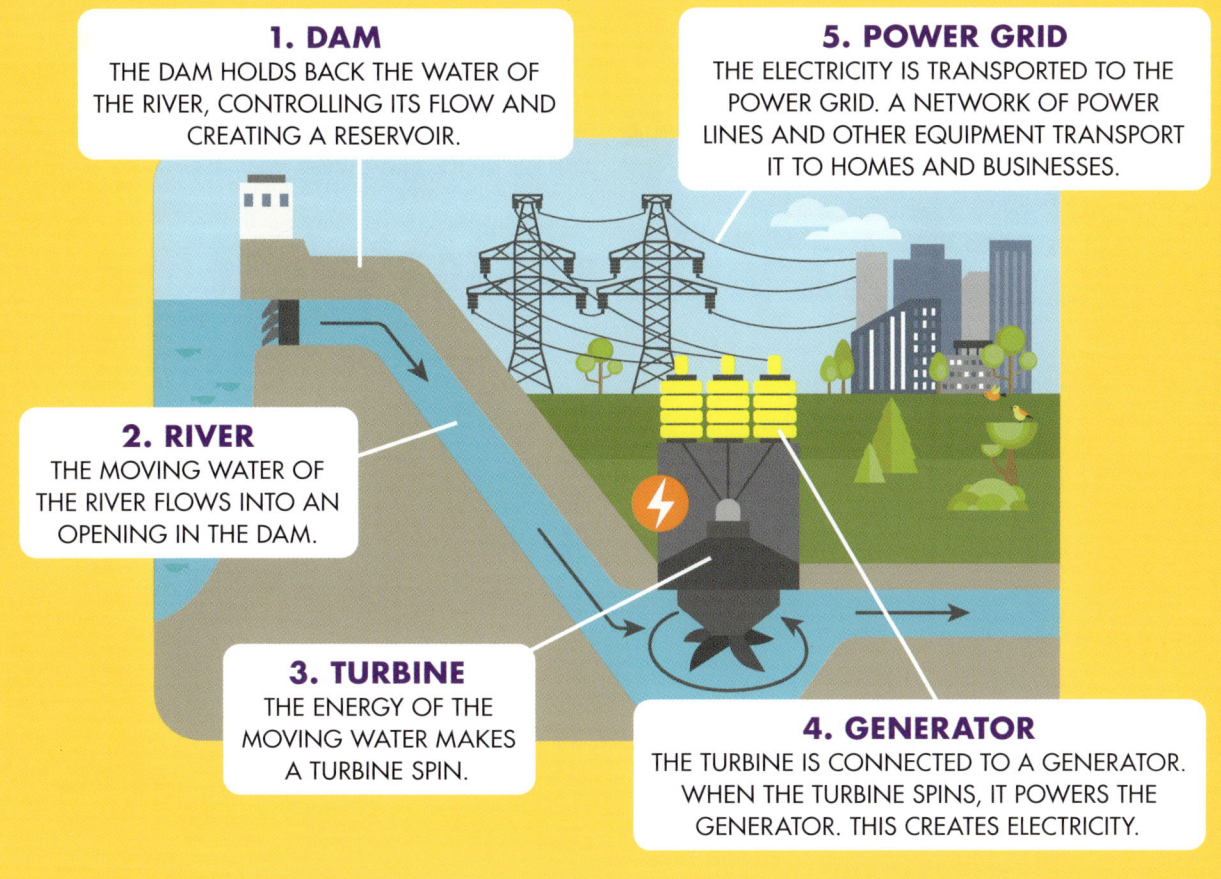

1. DAM
THE DAM HOLDS BACK THE WATER OF THE RIVER, CONTROLLING ITS FLOW AND CREATING A RESERVOIR.

2. RIVER
THE MOVING WATER OF THE RIVER FLOWS INTO AN OPENING IN THE DAM.

3. TURBINE
THE ENERGY OF THE MOVING WATER MAKES A TURBINE SPIN.

4. GENERATOR
THE TURBINE IS CONNECTED TO A GENERATOR. WHEN THE TURBINE SPINS, IT POWERS THE GENERATOR. THIS CREATES ELECTRICITY.

5. POWER GRID
THE ELECTRICITY IS TRANSPORTED TO THE POWER GRID. A NETWORK OF POWER LINES AND OTHER EQUIPMENT TRANSPORT IT TO HOMES AND BUSINESSES.

There are many steps to creating hydroelectric power.

In 2021, about 6.3 percent of the electricity in the United States was made using hydroelectric power. The electricity is used to power homes, schools, businesses, and more. It is one of the largest sources of renewable energy in the United States.

CHAPTER TWO

Positive Impacts of Hydropower

Hydropower is a renewable source of energy. Renewable resources are natural sources of energy. They will never run out. Nonrenewable resources can be used up. Examples of these are coal and oil. Using the energy of moving water does not reduce the amount of water on Earth. Instead, hydropower relies on the water cycle.

Hydropower is a source of clean energy. It does not burn **fossil fuels**. Burning fossil fuels emits greenhouse gases. These gases play a role in **climate change**. Also, hydropower is a safe source of energy. It does not pollute. And there is no chance of an oil spill or gas leak.

Hydropower plants are not expensive to run. Rising fossil fuel prices do not affect these plants either.

Hydropower created about 31.5 percent of all renewable electricity in the United States in 2021.

This keeps electrical bills low for people who use hydroelectric power.

Hydropower can be made in the United States. Water is found across the country. It does not need to be sent to the United States like other energy sources.

In fact, there are hydropower facilities in almost all states. One of the largest is the Hoover Dam. It sits on the Arizona-Nevada border on the Colorado River. It makes enough electricity for 1.3 million people each year. By using hydropower, the United States does not need to rely on other countries for energy sources.

Hydropower has other advantages, too. It is more reliable than other renewable resources, such as solar power and wind power. As long as there is water, power can be made 24 hours a day. And at dams, gates can be opened or closed. This controls when electricity is made. It also controls how much electricity is made. That means more energy can be created at times of greater demand.

THE WATER CYCLE

The water cycle plays an important role in hydropower. When the sun warms water in lakes, rivers, and oceans, the water evaporates. This means it changes from a liquid to a vapor. The vapor rises into the air. In the atmosphere, the vapor cools. It becomes a liquid again and forms clouds. Eventually it falls as precipitation. The water falls to the ground. It makes its way into streams and rivers. As the water runs downstream, it is used to generate hydropower.

In 2020, 25 percent of greenhouse gases in the United States came from burning fossil fuels, such as coal, for electricity.

The Hoover Dam is 726.4 feet (221.4 m) tall. When it was built in 1935, it was the tallest dam in the world. It had the largest hydroelectric plant in the world until 1948.

For example, hydropower can help restore the energy supply after a blackout. On-demand hydropower can be put into the **electrical grid** faster than other sources of energy. All of this improves the stability of the grid.

Hydropower may also be used with other renewable resources. Wind and solar power rely on the wind or sun. But these sources are not always available. During these times, hydropower is used to provide renewable energy.

Lake Mead is a reservoir created by the Hoover Dam. It is a popular spot for boating, water sports, and outdoor activities. About 25 million people also depend on Lake Mead as a source of drinking water.

Dams that create reservoirs have other benefits. For one, reservoirs collect and store drinking water. The stored water can also be used to water crops. Even in times of drought, clean fresh water is available. These reservoirs provide opportunities for fun, too. People can often use reservoirs for swimming, boating, and fishing.

CHAPTER THREE

Negative Impacts of Hydropower

Hydropower has negative impacts, too. One is its effect on the environment. When dams are built, they interrupt the natural flow of a river. Systems that redirect water also interrupt the flow. These interruptions affect fish migrations. Salmon, for example, swim upriver from the sea to reproduce. They must reach the place where they hatched years before. But dams and diversion systems block their way. Others are killed by turbines. As a result, the populations of salmon and other fish are falling.

Dams and reservoirs have other impacts. They change water temperature. They affect the amount and type of minerals and nutrients in the water. The amount of oxygen in the water downstream is lowered. Plus, all rivers carry sediment. This includes rocks, dirt, and sand.

Over the past 50 years, the number of migrating freshwater fish around the world has gone down by about 76 percent. Dams are one of the main reasons for this.

FISH LADDERS

Dams block the natural flow of rivers. They sometimes block migrating fish. To address this problem, people make fish ladders. A fish ladder is a detour around the dam. It is a man-made waterway made up of pools, each one higher than the one before it. As the fish migrate, they reach one pool. Then they leap upstream through falling water to the next higher pool. They rest. Then they leap up to the next higher pool. This mimics the movements they make in a natural river.

Sediment is important to the health of the whole river. It shapes the natural environment and carries nutrients. But dams and reservoirs trap a lot of sediment. As a result, the river downstream does not get the sediment it needs.

Dams also control the flow of water. When there is a drought, less water is released. This makes the drought worse downstream. Plants and animals do not get the water they need. People downstream have less water to use. The Colorado River is an example. It flows through seven western U.S. states. There are many dams along the river. The Hoover Dam and the Glen Canyon Dam are two of them. Much of the water is stored behind the dams. Some water is used for agriculture. The natural flow of the river has been greatly reduced by the dams.

The Colorado River is one of the most important water sources in the United States. But people have overused its water supply. Since 2000, the river's flow has gone down by about 20 percent. In some years, sections of the river have even dried up.

The Three Gorges Dam created a huge reservoir. It flooded two cities and 114 towns along the Yangtze River.

Low water levels along the Colorado River threaten animals like the bighorn sheep.

By the river's end, there is almost no flow. Native plants and animals are impacted. They do not get enough water.

Building dams affects people as well. The Three Gorges Dam was built on the Yangtze River in China. It is one of the largest dams in the world. It is 1.45 miles (2.3 km) across and 607 feet (185 m) tall. The dam created an artificial lake larger than New York City. It flooded hundreds of villages. More than one million people had to move. Countless historical sites were lost.

Experts have discovered that each year, man-made reservoirs give off more greenhouse gases than the entire country of Germany. About 79 percent of the gas released from reservoirs is methane.

Hydropower does not give off greenhouse gases. But the building of dams and reservoirs might. Making the materials needed to build a dam uses energy that may be generated using fossil fuels. Reservoirs behind dams also release greenhouse gases. Greenhouse gases form in both natural and man-made lakes. This happens as materials in the water decay. As they decay, they create gases. These gases are released into the atmosphere. But studies show that hydropower reservoirs give off more gases than natural lakes. Part of the reason is that reservoirs flood areas with plants. Once flooded, those plants decay.

Finally, hydropower needs water to work. It is often a reliable source of energy, but not always. Sometimes there are extended droughts. During those times, less water is available. Less water flowing through the plant means less electricity is made. Therefore, hydropower is affected by weather. If energy production is too low, communities must turn to other energy sources.

CHAPTER FOUR

The Future of Hydropower

Many people like the idea of using hydropower. Yet few new large-scale dams and reservoirs will be built in the United States. This is partly due to environmental concerns about dams and reservoirs. Also, as of 2022, dams had already been built on most of the useable spots for hydropower projects in the United States.

Instead, the industry is turning to existing dams that do not make electricity. There are more than 80,000 dams in the United States. Only 3 percent produce power. Nonpowered dams can be fitted with generators and turbines. Converting existing dams has no added environmental impacts. More clean, renewable energy can be made. This idea is supported by both environmentalists and the hydropower industry.

Most nonpowered dams in the United States were built to control floods, provide water for farmland, or help with navigation along rivers. Converting these dams could help stop new dams from being built.

In addition, more communities are using small plants to make power locally. Some small-scale systems move water from streams. The flow of water through hydropower turbines is used for power. And small existing dams are being fitted with generators and turbines.

Hydropower plants have tried to improve or create new pathways for migrating fish, such as fish ladders and fish lifts. With these pathways, more fish can pass through dams safely and travel down the river faster.

This small-scale approach has little impact on wildlife and the environment.

Other hydropower plants are getting upgrades. New technology and systems are being installed. This makes the plants more efficient. They can create more energy.

Also, oxygen can be added to water released from these dams. This provides more oxygen to the water downstream. Plus, new pathways around dams aid fish migration.

There is one other source of hydropower that engineers are looking into: the ocean. The waves of the ocean are a constant source of energy. Capturing the energy from waves works in much the same way as in a river. Underwater turbines are attached to buoys. The force of the waves spins the turbines. The spinning turbines then make electricity. Power lines deliver the electricity to the electrical grid.

Tides are another source of ocean energy. Energy is created as the tides rise and fall.

IS ENERGY FROM THE OCEAN THE WAVE OF THE FUTURE?

There are pros and cons to using the power of the ocean to make electricity. Both tidal currents and waves have the potential to generate enormous amounts of energy. They are also reliable. One of the greatest benefits is that they are a renewable resource. They do not give off greenhouse gases. However, there are environmental concerns. Marine wildlife is affected. Underwater turbines can take up space and create noise. This can alter animal habitats and even impact fish migrations. These systems are expensive and difficult to install, too.

Most tidal power stations create electricity with tidal turbines, tidal fences, or tidal barrages, which are similar to dams.

More than 1,000 years ago, this type of hydropower was used in Europe. People ran grain factories with tidal power. Tidal systems can also be used to make electricity. There are now tidal systems doing this in many countries. South Korea, France, and Canada have the world's largest tidal power systems.

The ocean has great potential to make electricity. However, capturing that energy is difficult. The salt water affects the equipment. Also, the ocean environment is often rough. Systems are still being developed and improved.

Hydropower is certain to play an important role in the future. But what that future will look like is still unclear. Scientists and engineers are working on environmentally friendly projects. The goal is for hydropower to provide clean, renewable energy into the future.

Glossary

climate change (KLYE-mit CHAYNJ) Climate change refers to long-term changes in global temperatures and weather patterns. Using hydropower could help fight climate change.

electrical grid (i-LEK-tri-kuhl GRID) The electrical grid is the system that produces and delivers electricity to users. Using hydropower makes the electrical grid more reliable.

fossil fuels (FOSS-uhl FYOO-uhls) Fossil fuels are sources of energy that come from the remains of plants and animals that died long ago. Coal, oil, and natural gas are examples of fossil fuels.

generator (JEN-uh-ray-tur) A generator is a machine that turns the rotational energy of a turbine into electrical energy. Hydropower plants use generators to turn moving water into electricity.

kinetic energy (ki-NET-ik EN-ur-jee) Kinetic energy is the energy of a moving object. Water moving down a river has kinetic energy.

reservoir (REZ-ur-vwar) A reservoir is a natural or man-made lake used to store large amounts of water. A reservoir is created when a dam is built.

turbines (TUR-bines) Turbines are machines driven by water, steam, or gas passing over blades on a wheel. The invention of turbines was a big advancement in the use of hydropower.

Fast Facts

- People have used hydropower for more than 2,000 years.
- One of the earliest tools used to generate hydropower was the waterwheel.
- Hydropower is a renewable resource and a clean source of energy.
- Hydropower systems are reliable and inexpensive once installed.
- The building of dams and reservoirs impacts wildlife and the environment.
- Nonpowered dams in the United States may be turned into power-generating dams.
- Engineers are working on using the energy of tides and waves to produce electricity.

One Stride Further

- Do you support building more hydroelectric dams? Write a paragraph explaining why or why not.
- Hydropower has environmental impacts. What are some ways to reduce those impacts?
- Do you think that the positives of hydropower outweigh the negatives? Explain.
- Considering the need for clean renewable energy and the environmental impacts of hydropower, what do you think the future of hydropower will look like?

Find Out More

IN THE LIBRARY

Brearley, Laurie. *Water Power: Energy from Rivers, Waves, and Tides.* New York, NY: Children's Press, 2019.

Doeden, Matt. *Finding Out about Hydropower.* Minneapolis, MN: Lerner, 2015.

Sneideman, Joshua, and Erin Twamley. *Renewable Energy: Discover the Fuel of the Future with 20 Projects.* White River Junction, VT: Nomad Press, 2016.

ON THE WEB

Visit our website for links about hydroelectric power: **childsworld.com/links**

Note to Parents, Teachers, and Librarians: We routinely verify our Web links to make sure they are safe and active sites. So encourage your readers to check them out!

Index

fish migrations, 16–17, 18, 26–27

fossil fuels, 10, 13, 23

greenhouse gases, 10, 13, 22–23, 27

Hoover Dam, 8, 12, 14–15, 18

hydroelectric plants, 6–9, 10–12, 14, 24–25, 26–27

reservoirs, 7–9, 15, 16, 18, 20–21, 22–23, 24

turbines, 4, 6, 7–9, 16, 24–25, 27–28